MONSTER
AND THE BABY

MONSTER AND THE BABY

Virginia Mueller

pictures by Lynn Munsinger

Puffin Books

PUFFIN BOOKS
Published by the Penguin Group
Viking Penguin Inc., 40 West 23rd Street, New York, New York 10010, U.S.A.
Penguin Books Ltd, 27 Wrights Lane, London W8 5TZ England
Penguin Books Australia Ltd, Ringwood, Victoria, Australia
Penguin Books Canada Ltd, 2801 John Street, Markham, Ontario, Canada L3R 1B4
Penguin Books (N.Z.) Ltd, 182–190 Wairau Road, Auckland 10, New Zealand

Penguin Books Ltd, Registered Offices: Harmondsworth, Middlesex, England

First published in the United States of America by Albert Whitman & Company, 1985
Published in Picture Puffins 1988
1   3   5   7   9   10   8   6   4   2
Text copyright © Virginia Mueller, 1985
Illustrations copyright © Lynn Munsinger, 1985
All rights reserved
Printed in Hong Kong by South China Printing Company
Set in Helvetica

Library of Congress Cataloging in Publication Data
Mueller, Virginia.
Monster and the baby/Virginia Mueller; pictures by Lynn Munsinger
p. cm.—(Picture puffins)
Summary: Trying to entertain his baby brother by building a tower
out of blocks, Monster finds there is only one way to stop him from crying.
ISBN 0-14-050880-5
[1. Babies—Fiction.   2. Brothers—Fiction.   3. Monsters—
Fiction.]   I. Munsinger, Lynn. ill.   II. Title.
[PZ7.M879Mo 1988]   [E]—dc19   88-11706

For Amy, Mike, and Sarah *V. M.*
For Rachel *L. M.*

Baby was crying.

Monster gave Baby one red block.

Baby cried.

Monster gave Baby two yellow blocks.

Baby cried.

Monster gave Baby three blue blocks.

Baby cried.

Monster put the three blue blocks on the bottom,

the two yellow blocks in the middle,

and the one red block on the top.

Monster hit the blocks!

Baby laughed and laughed.